ANCIENT GREEK MYTHS

MINOTAUR

Author
Gilly Cameron Cooper

Consultant
Nick Saunders

Copyright © ticktock Entertainment Ltd 2007
First published in Great Britain in 2007 by ticktock Media Ltd.,
Unit 2, Orchard Business Centre, North Farm Road,
Tunbridge Wells, Kent, TN2 3XF

ticktock project editor: Jo Hanks
ticktock project designer: Graham Rich

We would like to thank: Indexing Specialists (UK) Ltd.

ISBN 978 1 84696 065 9
Printed in China
A CIP catalogue record for this book is available from the British Library.

CONTENTS

THE GREEKS, THEIR GODS & MYTHS

The ancient Greeks lived in a world dominated by the Mediterranean Sea, the snow-capped mountains that surrounded it, dangerous winds, and sudden storms. They saw their lives as controlled by the gods and spirits of Nature, and told myths about how the gods fought with each other and created the universe.

It was a world of chance and luck, of magic and superstition, in which the endless myths made sense of a dangerous and unpredictable life.

The ancient Greek gods looked and acted like human beings. They fell in love, were jealous, vain, and argued with each other. Unlike humans, they were immortal. This meant they did not die, but lived forever. They also had superhuman strength and magical powers. Each god had a power that belonged only to them.

In the myths, the gods sometimes had children with humans. These children were born demi-gods and might have special powers, but were usually mortal and could die. When their human children were in trouble, the Olympian gods would help them.

The gods liked to meddle in to human life. Different gods took sides with different people. The gods also liked to play tricks on humans. They did this for all sorts of reasons: because it was fun; because

they would gain something; and also for revenge. The Ancient Greeks believed that 12 Olympian gods ruled over the world at any time. The gods and goddesses that you see here were always Olympians, they were the most important ones. Some of them you'll meet in our story.

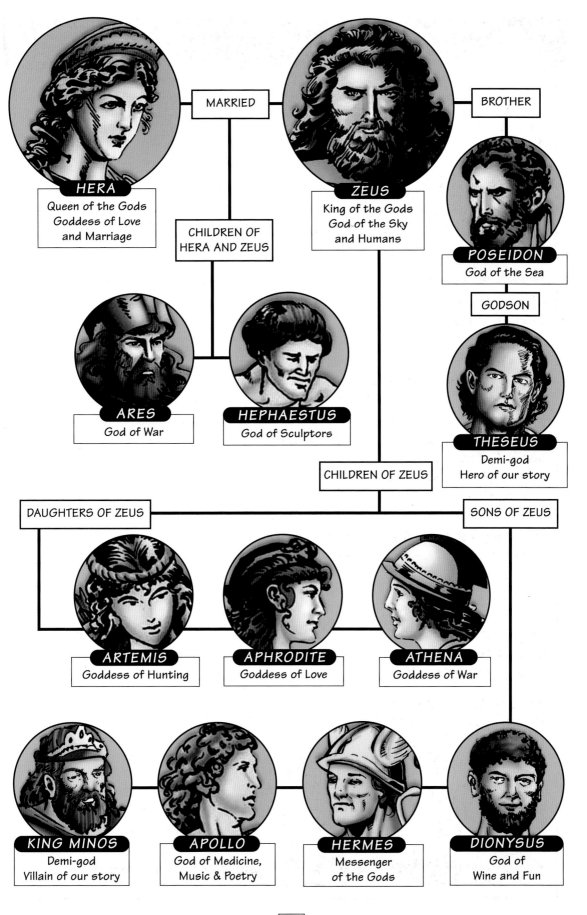

HERA
Queen of the Gods
Goddess of Love
and Marriage

MARRIED

ZEUS
King of the Gods
God of the Sky
and Humans

BROTHER

POSEIDON
God of the Sea

CHILDREN OF
HERA AND ZEUS

ARES
God of War

HEPHAESTUS
God of Sculptors

GODSON

THESEUS
Demi-god
Hero of our story

CHILDREN OF ZEUS

DAUGHTERS OF ZEUS

SONS OF ZEUS

ARTEMIS
Goddess of Hunting

APHRODITE
Goddess of Love

ATHENA
Goddess of War

KING MINOS
Demi-god
Villain of our story

APOLLO
God of Medicine,
Music & Poetry

HERMES
Messenger
of the Gods

DIONYSUS
God of
Wine and Fun

SETTING THE SCENE

The two most powerful men in this story were demi-gods. This means that they had one parent who was a god, and another who was a human. Theseus had two human parents but was also the godson of the sea-god Poseidon. King Minos of Crete had Zeus, king of the gods, for a father. King Minos was the most powerful and wealthy ruler of Greece at the time of this story. His palace was on the island of Crete. From here, King Minos controlled the most important trade routes in the Mediterranean. The rest of Greece at this time was made up of small kingdoms that had no stable rule and little money. This made it easy for the Minoans to call the shots, and demand money from weaker states.

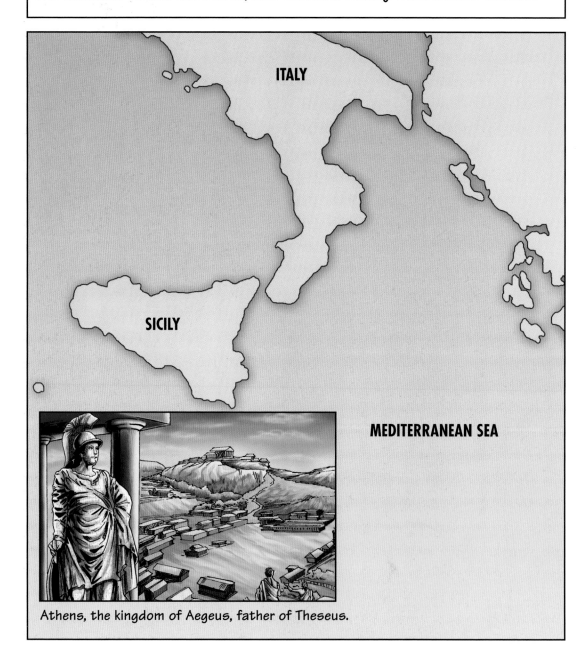

ITALY

SICILY

MEDITERRANEAN SEA

Athens, the kingdom of Aegeus, father of Theseus.

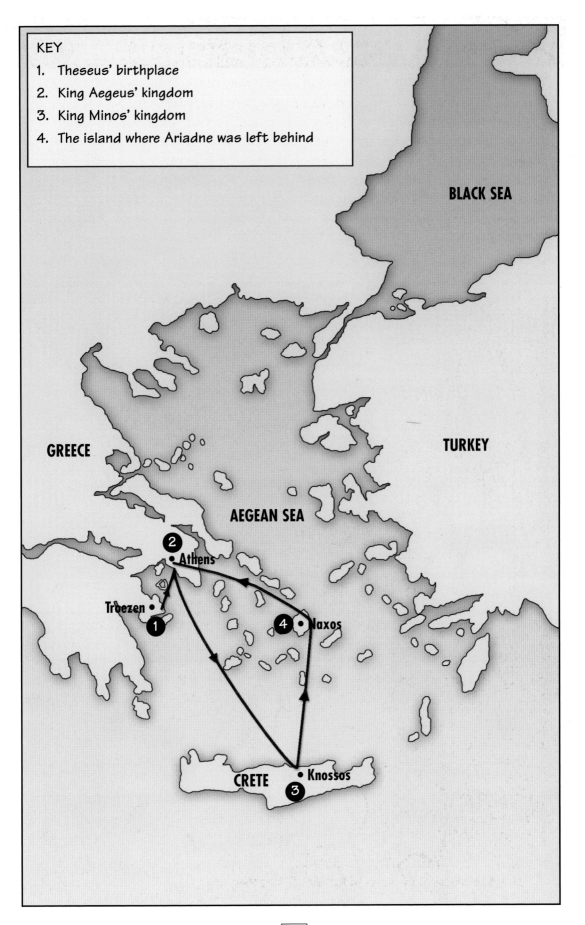

KEY
1. Theseus' birthplace
2. King Aegeus' kingdom
3. King Minos' kingdom
4. The island where Ariadne was left behind

BLACK SEA

GREECE

TURKEY

AEGEAN SEA

② ●Athens

Troezen ●

①

④ ●Naxos

CRETE ●Knossos

③

BIRTH OF A HERO

Theseus' parents were Aegeus, king of Athens, and Princess Aethra of Troezen. This meant that Theseus would inherit the throne of Athens. The couple weren't together for long. Aegeus had to return to Athens, which was being torn apart by fighting between different groups of people. The night Aegeus left, Aethra went to Poseidon's temple. Poseidon was lord of the sea and guardian god of Troezen. Poseidon agreed to become godfather to Aethra's unborn child.

Bring our child up here, in secret. It would be too dangerous for him in Athens. My brother's sons would kill a son of mine, to stop him having my throne.

Their child will be great, and worthy of my protection.

Aegeus asked Aethra to hide his sandals and a dagger under a large rock. He went back to Athens. Nine months later, Theseus was born.

Princess Aethra would not say who Theseus' father was. People thought he must be Poseidon's son. When Theseus was older, Aethra decided he was ready for the truth.

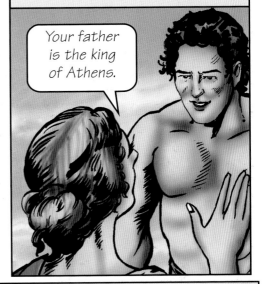

Your father is the king of Athens.

Aethra told Theseus about the rock where his father's sandals and dagger were hidden.

I must go to my father in Athens and claim my place as his son and heir. These will help him recognise me.

Theseus could have sailed straight to Athens, but he wanted to prove he was brave. So, he took the long road to Athens that was riddled with dangerous villains.

Very soon, Theseus met a bandit who crushed anyone who crossed his path with a huge spiked club. Theseus tackled and defeated him. He then seized the weapon and battered the man to death with it. Theseus kept the club, it was to come in very useful...

The next problem for Theseus was a man known as 'Pine-bender'. He would pull together a couple of trees, then tie people between them. The trees sprang back and the victims were torn apart. Our hero overpowered Pine-bender and got rid of him forever.

Theseus then came to a narrow path at the top of a high cliff. Far below, waves crashed against the rocks. A mean-looking man blocked his way. This man forced people to wash his feet. As soon as they bent down to do it, he kicked them over the cliff. In the sea below a giant flesh-eating turtle was waiting to eat them. Theseus picked the man up and threw him over the cliff.

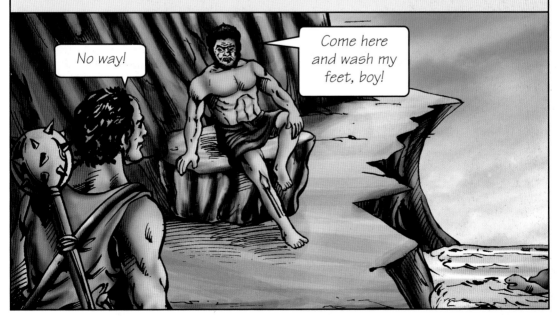

WELCOME TO ATHENS

News of Theseus' adventures and strength reached Athens. A feast was held for him at the palace. King Aegeus, now an old man, had married another woman called Medea. Together they had a son. Medea instantly knew who Theseus was, and that he would get in the way of her son becoming king. She told Aegeus that Theseus was dangerous, and he should poison his wine.

A chance soon arose for Theseus to impress the Athenians. For many years, a fire-breathing bull had brought terror to them, killing people by the hundreds. One of its first victims had been the son of the most powerful king in the Aegean, Minos of Crete…

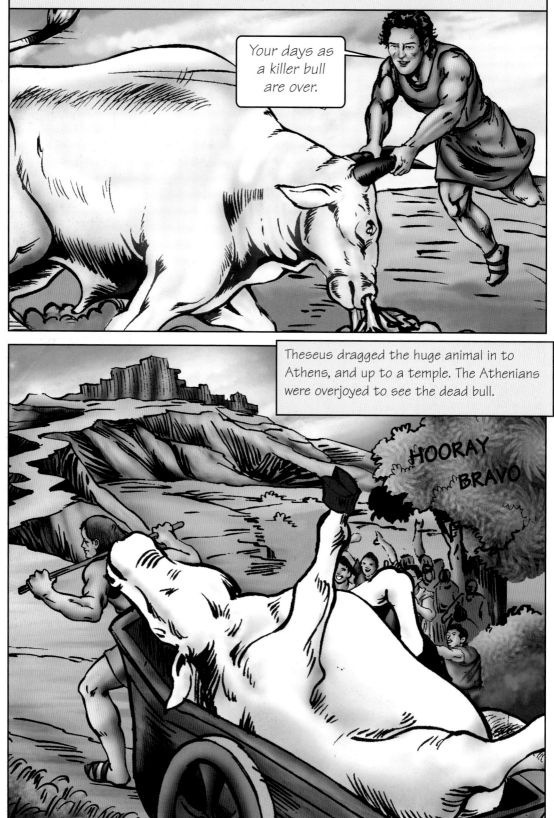

Your days as a killer bull are over.

Theseus dragged the huge animal in to Athens, and up to a temple. The Athenians were overjoyed to see the dead bull.

HOORAY

BRAVO

Theseus decided to sacrifice the bull as a gift to the goddess Athena. She was important to Athens, because she protected the city.

Why couldn't you have come sooner Theseus? This bull killed the son of King Minos. He blames us Athenians for it. We have to pay him back every year.

What? How?

MANY YEARS BEFORE...on the island of Crete, far to the south, King Minos received news that his son was dead. He blamed the Athenians.

My son died on Athenian soil. I shall make them pay for my loss with their own blood. They'll find out what it's like to lose their children.

Minos demanded payment for for his son's death. Every nine years the Athenians had to send 14 of their best young men and women to Crete. They were then killed by Crete's very own bull-monster, the dreaded Minotaur.

THE CHOSEN FEW

Just after Theseus' arrival in Athens, it was time for the third payment. King Minos sailed from Crete to make sure that the Athenians offered its best young people. They nervously gathered with their parents in the city square. They drew lots to decide who would go to Crete. Their parents were furious that King Aegeus' son Theseus was not taking part.

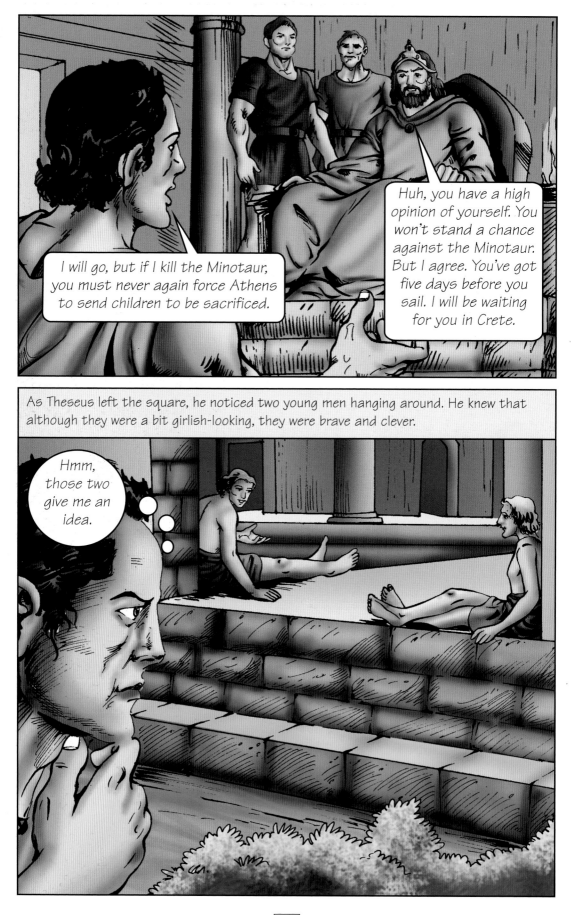

I will go, but if I kill the Minotaur, you must never again force Athens to send children to be sacrificed.

Huh, you have a high opinion of yourself. You won't stand a chance against the Minotaur. But I agree. You've got five days before you sail. I will be waiting for you in Crete.

As Theseus left the square, he noticed two young men hanging around. He knew that although they were a bit girlish-looking, they were brave and clever.

Hmm, those two give me an idea.

On the 6th of April, the chosen boys and girls gathered in the square, quiet and crying. The two brave boys, disguised as girls, joined the victims. Theseus grabbed a couple of the real chosen girls.

Quick, run home and hide. Your places will be taken by these two. Don't tell anyone!

Thank you so much!

Theseus led the 14 young people and their mothers to a temple to pray.

Please protect us.

The Minotaur sounds awful, we're all going to die.

The sad group dragged their feet as they went to the waiting ship.

The mothers brought baskets of food and fruit for the journey. They told their frightened children stories of heroes and heroines, to give them courage.

Be brave children. The monster might not be as awful as you think.

21

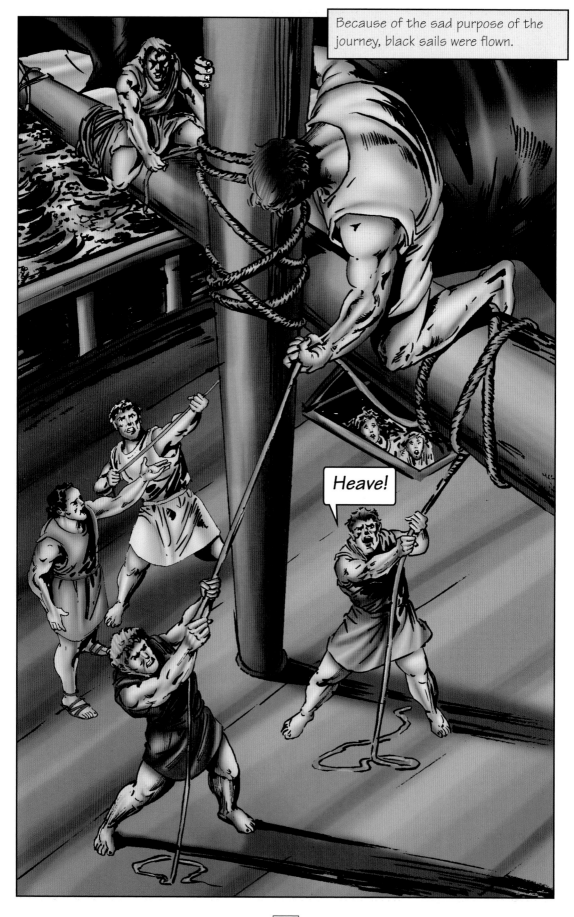

Just before they were about to leave, King Aegeus came aboard. With him were two servants carrying a white sail.

My son, may your godfather Poseidon look after you! Take this white sail and fly it on your return. Then I will know that you have killed the Minotaur and come home alive.

The ship set off. It was several days' journey to Crete. Something told Theseus that he should pray to the goddess of love, Aphrodite, to guide him. How could she help?

Theseus I hear your prayer. I don't know if I can help you, but I will try.

THE FIRST CHALLENGE

Theseus and his companions were amazed by Knossos, the capital of Crete. The buildings and the clothes that people wore were so much smarter than in Athens. Overlooking the town was a big palace. They could see King Minos being carried down to them. He wanted to make sure that all fourteen victims had arrived. Filled with fear, the boys and girls prepared to land.

Minos counted and checked the Athenians. He didn't notice the two boys disguised as girls. Maybe this was because his eyes had stopped on one, very pretty girl.

The king ordered to be set down at once. He was stiff after sitting in the chair and staggered to his feet. He wanted this girl for himself, even though he already had a wife.

Once the sky was clear again, Theseus plunged into the water. Dolphins immediately came to help Theseus, guiding him through the water. On the quay, Princess Ariadne, the lovely daughter of King Minos, was watching.

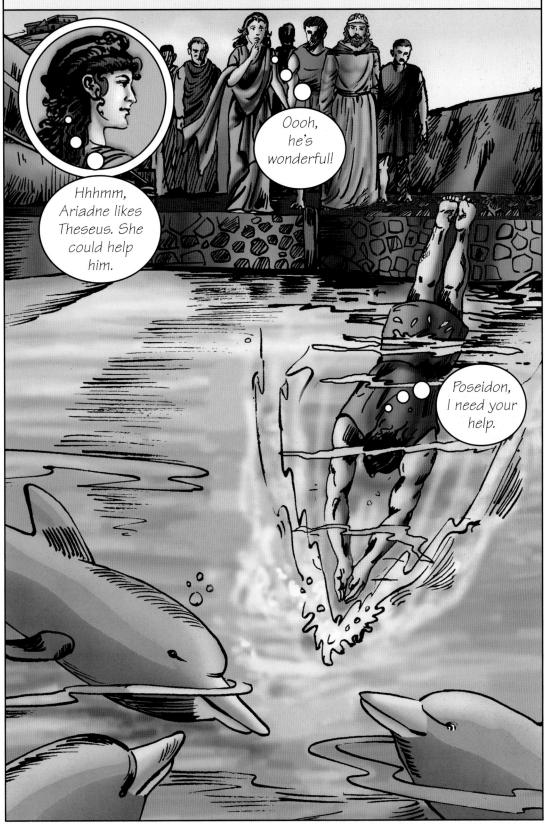

Poseidon sent his queen, Amphitrite and her sea-nymphs, to search for the ring. They found it lying between rocks. Amphitrite also gave Theseus a beautiful crown of delicate gold leaves. It had been her wedding present from the goddess of love, Aphrodite. It was extra proof that Poseidon was Theseus' godfather.

I think I can see something glittering.

We must find the ring quickly.

Here's my proof, King Minos.

Theseus burst out of the water, holding up the ring and the crown.

When Ariadne puts that crown on she will fall deeply in love with Theseus.

Here's your ring, and a sea-goddess' crown for your lovely daughter.

By Aphrodite, I love this incredible man. I must help him.

LOVERS UNITE

King Minos ordered his guards to take Theseus and the 13 others to his palace. A massive sculpture of bull horns above the main entrance reminded them of what was to come. The floors of the courtyard and rooms were covered in smooth black stone. The prisoners were taken away to be locked in a room. Ariadne bribed one of the guards so she could talk to Theseus.

Ariadne explained that the Minotaur lived in the centre of a labyrinth. It was a maze of false turns and secret passages, people got lost in it and died. She had some magic thread that Theseus must tie to the entrance of the labyrinth. The thread never ran out and would lead Theseus back out of the labyrinth. Asterius the Minotaur lived in the centre, to get to him Theseus must only make left turns.

Theseus decided to go into the labyrinth immediately. He was allowed to take his club, as no-one expected him to get out alive anyway. Theseus pushed open the labyrinth door and stepped into the dark.

All around Theseus were high walls that twisted and turned in a muddle of paths and dead-ends. Every direction looked the same. He felt the walls were closing in on him. At every junction, he followed Ariadne's instructions and turned left, never right. Sometimes he stumbled over the bones of other people who had not found their way out. He kept checking that the magic thread was unravelling behind him.

Theseus heard loud snores and smelled foul breath before he at last reached the heart of the labyrinth.

Finally Theseus stumble into a courtyard. At the side was Asterius, asleep. He was a huge man with a massive bull's head. Theseus knew that those deadly horns had ripped out the insides of many Athenian girls and boys.

What a disgusting creature.

Theseus crept up to the sleeping bull and grabbed its forelock and pulled.

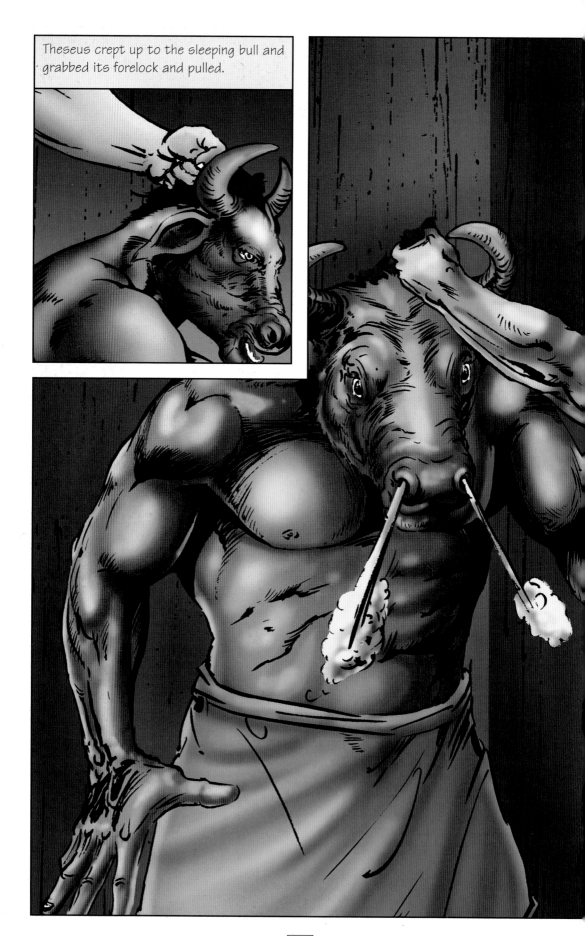

The Minotaur awoke and leapt to his feet with a wild roar. Theseus clung on to its forelock, and was whipped above the monster's head.

Suddenly, Theseus let go and flew through the air, did a neat backflip, and landed on his feet.

The Minotaur was so surprised, that it only took Theseus one blow with his famous club to kill the monster outright.

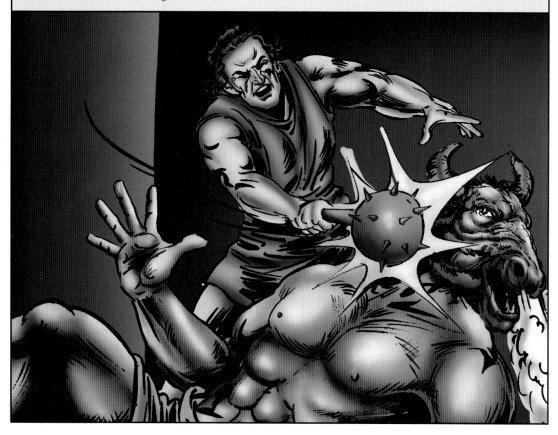

To please his godfather, Theseus immediately offered the bull as a sacrifice to Poseidon. Theseus then cut off the bull's head, and followed the thread all the way out of the labyrinth.

STEALTHY ESCAPE

While Theseus was in the labyrinth, the two boys disguised as girls had freed themselves and the other captives. The guards were caught completely by surprise when a couple of, what looked like, girls suddenly leapt on them. The boys took the guards' weapons, and killed them.

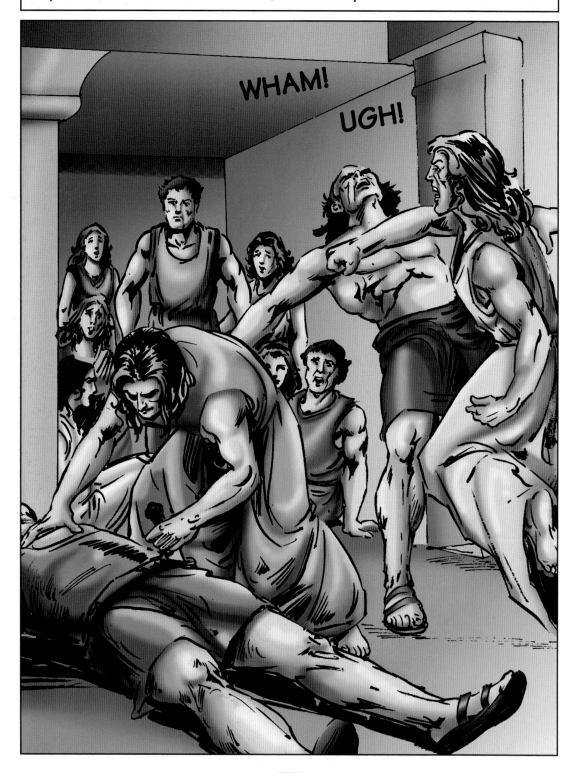

They rowed the ship, for fear of waking anyone. The thirty oars cut silently through the smooth black waters until they were safely away.

After several days of sailing, a storm forced the ship onto the island of Naxos. It was late and they decided to rest on the island until the storm passed.

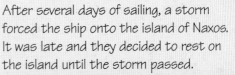

They awoke the next morning to good weather. Theseus was keen to set sail again, and went to check the ship. The others were awake too, and followed him. But Ariadne was comfortable on the soft grass and slept on.

The god of wine, Dionysus, cast a spell on Theseus to make him forget that Ariadne ever existed.

ARIADNE'S REVENGE

Eventually, the sleeping Ariadne stirred. She rubbed her eyes and yawned. Then her stomach lurched when she realised she was completely alone. Faraway, out to sea, there was a little black-sailed ship. Theseus had left her! Not only had she been cruelly dumped, but also abandoned on a strange and unknown island.

Meanwhile, the ship carrying Theseus and the others was close to Athens. Everyone was looking forward to being home.

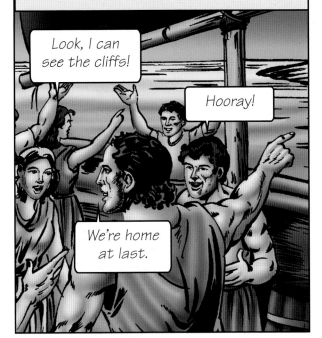

On shore stood King Aegeus. He had been looking out to sea every day, waiting for the white sail that would signal the safe return of Theseus.

But Theseus had forgotten to fly the white sail.

Thinking that his son was dead, Aegeus threw himself over the cliff to his death, in the sea below. That was how the gods punished Theseus for leaving behind Ariadne. They took away the father that Theseus had only just found.

The ship landed and Theseus led the way off, with the two disguised boys. As the celebrations began, no-one could bring themselves to tell Theseus of his father's death.

As soon as the parade was over, Theseus was told of his father's tragic death. He was very sad and built a shrine to the old king.

Theseus agreed to rule in his father's place. He became King of Athens and was a wise ruler. He brought together the different, fighting groups in Athens, and kept enemies away.

As for Ariadne, she married the god Dionysus. They had many children and lived happily on the beautiful island of Naxos. Dionysus was so happy that he blessed the island. Even today it is the greenest island in the Cyclades.

Bandit: *a violent criminal, who often steals from other people.*

City-state: *a centre of population with its own leader, laws and government. A city-state could be little more than a village and surrounding lands, or a big powerful fortified city such as Mycenae.*

Civilisation: *the stage of society when people have settled in towns and cities, have laws, art and music.*

Courage: *being able to do something that scares you.*

Cyclades: *a group of islands in the southern Aegean Sea, of which Naxos is the largest.*

Feast: *a celebration for a particular reason, such as someone's birthday. It usually involves lots of food and drink.*

Forelock: *a lock of hair that grows just above the forehead.*

Guardian god: *a god that is chosen or believed to have a special responsibility for protecting a place or a person.*

God-parent: *a person who is chosen to look after a child that is not their own.*

Harbour: *a place on the coast where ships can stop.*

Heir: *the person who has been chosen to receive the property, money or title (such as king) of a person who has died. Children are often the heirs to their parents' property.*

Immortal: *living forever, with no death, like the gods.*

Inherit: *to receive property, money or title (such as king) on someone's death.*

Knossos: *the place on the island of Crete where King Minos had his palace and the capital of the Minoan civilisation.*

Labyrinth: *a maze or confusing network of passages or paths in which it is difficult to find your way.*

Lottery: *a random selection of numbers.*

Minoan: *A civilisation named after its most famous king, Minos and centred on the island of Crete in the southern Aegean Sea. Minoan power was based on successful trade and great wealth. It was the first civilisation and the first one to have a form of writing, in Europe. It came after the early Mesopotamian* and Egyptian civilisations.

Mission: *an important job that is sometimes secret.*

Mortal: *having a life that is ended by death, usually referring to humans as distinct from immortal gods.*

Myths: *the stories of a tribe or people that tell of their gods, heroes and turning points in their history.*

Olympian: *describes the 12 Greek gods who lived on Mount Olympus in northern Greece, headed by Zeus, and including Poseidon and Athena.*

Qualify: *meet certain conditions to take part in a competition.*

Quay: *a platform where ships land, and can load or unload.*

Revenge: *Getting your own back on someone who has harmed you, or for someone you care about.*

Shrine: *a holy place, dedicated to one particular god.*

Temple: *a building where gods are worshipped.*

Villain: *a criminal.*

INDEX